THE DEFINITION OF WAHR

A YOUNG ADULT ROMANCE

MELISSA BELL

For my Family

ACKNOWLEDGMENTS

Editor
J.J. Jarret

BLURB

In a fantastical time of Kings who thought they were Gods and Gods who believed they were Kings.

There was one who stood with a foot in both worlds.

To his father, 'Zion,' his son is the son of a God, but to his mother, 'Ezla,' he's the future king of the Seelies.

What does a demigod do when he falls in love with the princess of a rival faction?

PROLOGUE

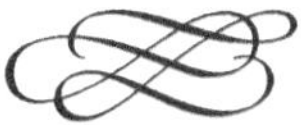

"As the Queen of the Seelie Court, I will not permit you to take my son and our future king to your realm," Ezla scorned Zion. "If I need to protect him from your world, I will banish you from ours."

"Ezla, my love, he will need my guidance as he grows. He is the son of a God, and my blood runs in his veins. You will never be able to prevent me from reaching out to him. Even if it is through his thoughts," Zion glanced at the bundle in Ezla's arms. "Will you let me hold him?"

"Are you insane?" Ezla frowned harshly at him.

It was easy to identify why he'd been so drawn to her. She was fierce in facing off against a god with the power to erase not only the Queen of the Seelie but the entire race. Regardless, it didn't seem to faze her. Ezla had more important things to deal with. She knew the instant the Unseelie heard about the birth of their son; they would surely attempt to come for him.

Sudden screeching beyond the veil of vines was the only warning Ezla needed, "Protect our son!" she commanded Zion. In a shimmer of blue light, Ezla was instantly dressed, ready to meet with the cause of the torturous sounds.

The wind chimes and bells warned the Seelie Court of how important it was to stay vigilant against the Unseelies.

Zion wrapped his son in the balance of his cloak, with his lips brushing against the shell of his son's ear, he whispered. "If I were the beings making that raucous, I would be fearful of your mother. Queen Ezla is a force to be reckoned with, even at her weakest, I would hazard a guess that she could silence the calls of a Banshee to protect you."

CHAPTER 1

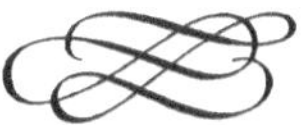

Boom – Boom – Ting – Boom Shk Shk – Boom – Ding dinga ding Boom Boom – Shk Shk.

The industrial sound of the music resonated all the way down to his soul. His hips swayed, and he played the tempo with both hands in the air as though he possessed drumsticks. He was taller than the average male on the dance floor, and when he opened his eyes, it was to discover all the women desperately trying to make eye contact with him.

Wahr refused them all, focusing instead on the men surrounding him with the full intention of causing him harm.

Honestly, he couldn't care less about the human females searching for the attention of the only male in sight that didn't have two left feet.

As the song changed, he did a slow turn, keeping in rhythm with the doof-doof beat. He'd managed to stay under the radar for at least twenty minutes, which would surmount to about a week back home.

The blonde guy to his left was the first one to make a move. His girlfriend was trying to hold his arm back from following through on his punch. Wahr captured his fist in his palm and reversing its momentum he added to its force. On impact, that one squealed like a girl as his lip split open on his teeth. After that, the club aptly named 'Pandemonium' erupted into the true sense of its name.

As Wahr stepped out of the club with the escort of the bouncers, he spun on his heal and saluted them, "Till next time, boys."

The tuff stuff on the right scrunched his face up and shook his head to indicate that it wasn't likely to be any time soon. The dark-haired goon on the left pulled out his phone and pointed it in Wahr's direction, taking a snapshot. When he lowered the device, he frowned, flicking through the camera roll. "Hey, Justin, did you see that?" Brandon asked the other bouncer. Wahr had been burned at every club he'd been to in the past two months, thankfully none of them could withstand his trickery.

"See what, man?" Justin responded, turning his head to look at the images on Brandon's phone. "Oh, hey, is that your new ride?" he asked when he spotted a photo of an old Mustang. "Man that's sweet, how long do you think it will take to restore that bad boy?"

"Hmm," Brandon looked around as if he had been doing something important. "A year or two, maybe. It depends on how quickly I can locate the parts to restore her."

Justin puzzled, "Why do they always refer to cars as female?"

"I have no idea, man, but my Mustang is all beef. There is nothing feminine about that car."

"If you say so, dude. Whatever, did you see where I put my phone?"

Wahr shook his head and pushed off of the wall he was leaning on to walk across the street.

As the toe of Wahr's boot touched the edge of the grass, his glamour slid away as he slipped through the veil, separating his world from that of the humans. The time taken was less than three seconds. However, for others, it was probably more like three days of pain and suffering. It was most likely why they were forever receiving warnings against traveling to the place the Seelie's whispered about, 'Meridian.' The world between his mother's native lands and that of his father's.

Wahr knew the sylphs would inform his mother as soon as he arrived on the other side of the veil. He sighed as he landed smack dab in the middle of the Unseelie patrol of the Northern regions.

He really should be more careful, but he had been given his name for a reason, and legends had been written long before his mother's, mother was born. It was foretold of a male Seelie that would erase an entire race. He guessed that's why all of the fae, both benevolent and nefarious alike, were reluctant to cross his path.

His pouch beeped, and the Unseelie's looked in his direction as if they hadn't noticed his presence prior to a sound they'd never heard before but still knew what it was from the lessons of aging.

Wahr pulled the offending device from where he'd stashed it after re-moving it from the back pocket of Justin's pants. It repeated its desire for attention. The screen flashing a signal, 'No Service,' whatever that meant? When he looked up from the piece of technol-ogy, it was to find himself completely alone. He shrugged, figuring it was prob-ably for the best considering the tales. For a brief moment, he considered turning tail and returning to the place he'd just returned from. Before he could make that choice, a blue clicker landed on his chest, it quickly scurried under his armor, preventing him from flat out squashing it like the poisonous bug it was to his people. He shook his head, 'My people?' who exactly were his people? Half-Seelie and half-god. His mother's people feared him, and his father's refused to acknowledge him. He had been testing theories with every adventure into the human world.

He'd collected items and souvenirs such as silver, iron, salt, sugar, and now technological equipment. He also discovered that he enjoyed the hot refreshment of the human's called coffee, but decided that it definitely tasted better with cream and sugar.

He'd made the harsh error of drinking it black while visiting a Meridian Beverage house. The female table attendant had placed a cup before him and poured a hot black liquid into it. The aroma wasn't unpleasant to his nose, so he lifted it to his lips, taking a large mouthful, not expecting the oral assault to be so violent. It burned his tongue like hot acid, and its bitter aftertaste caused him to push the offensive offering away. The woman returned a short time later to refill his cup with the tarlike substance, but after noticing that he hadn't touched it past the initial sip, she asked, "Would you like sugar and cream with that?" After careful consideration, he gave a nod, concluding it couldn't be any worse than his first attempt at blending in. His reaction had been so unexpected that his glamour had faltered, only briefly, but still, it was a danger to his kind. It was bad enough that he'd been confronted with the knowledge that others were being used for entertainment. Vampires were a predator where he came from.

On this side of the veil, they were pop fiction right beside the shifters and werewolves. What had become of the human world once that storyteller had written about Avalon was beyond reversible.

With a healthy dose of experimentation on his part, he'd established that because of his parentage, he wasn't like the other Seelie's. He could wear silver. He could touch iron without becoming weakened or sickly. He'd sat at the table in the diner and played with the spilled sugar without the compulsion to count it. Sure it had been mesmerizing to draw patterns in the pile of salt he emptied from the caddy until the waitress stopped to clean it up. It was interesting to discover that humans were a superstitious creed, as he'd watched the female toss a pinch salt over her left shoulder. Since the addition of the sugar and cream, he'd become almost addicted to the coffee served to patrons in the middle of the dark times in the human world. That was another thing that he found fascinating, the light and dark times in Meridian. If he were to consider ever leaving his world for this one, then he would have to learn to adapt to it.

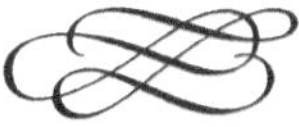

"Oreodaphne, you will come to the Unseelie Court to accept your fate," the male voice demanded.

Oreo hated it when anyone used her full name in an attempt to put her in her place. She'd been consistently avoiding doing what she was expected to do most of her life. The idea of conforming make her feel sickly at the slightest thought of it. "Not today Zayton," she put her hand up into the face of the male her parents had decreed she be harnessed to for all of eternity.

As the Princess of the Unseelie's, if she were to become Queen one day, then she at least wanted to have someone she liked standing at her side. At the first signs of any dissatisfaction or confrontation, Zayton ran for the closest place to vanish and hide. Oreo wanted to have a male she could rely on, depend on and converse with, not one who she suspected was more inclined to slice her throat while she slept.

A shift in the air behind Zayton and the Unseelie guard drew her attention. Leaning to one side, she aimed to glimpse the origination of the gleaming. Oreo's eyes widened when she blinked twice before the male moved quickly to silence the noise coming from his satchel. The moment the distraction took the focal point away from her and onto the Seelie who had just broken any number of laws put in place by the Seelie Queen, Oreo disappeared from sight. Oh, she may not be visible, but that didn't mean she wasn't standing amongst the center of the action. She stepped around the Unseelie Guards without touching any of them, no matter how tempted she was to poke Zayton in the eye on her way past him. He was such a lowly creature; she was almost certain he had horns.

Everything happened so quickly it was as though she had only blinked once. One moment she was being challenged by Zayton, and the next, she was all alone. Well, other than the Seelie, who was presently watching a Blue Clicker, desperately looking for a place to get lost under his armor.

Wahr narrowed his eyes and surveyed his surroundings, although the Unseelie's had evacuated the area, he knew he wasn't alone. Turning his head slowly from one side to the other, he paused momentarily to close his eyes to center his core. His hand shot out in the same instant as his eyes snapped open. His top lip curled in a sign of distaste towards the invader of his private contemplation. Wahr's fingers surrounded soft flesh, and although his grip was firm, it wasn't brutal.

Oreo wondered if the brutish brog was aware that his killing her would actually be a positive move in the right direction as far as she was concerned. Anything had to be better than being anchored to Zayton.

'Snapdragons chasing glitter -bugs!' she thought as her surroundings began to lose color.

The Seelie's hair was no longer stark black but a washed-out dirty grey. And his green queen's guard threads were a middle of the range grey. With a quick glance around, there had to be at least fifty shades of grey.

Her eyes began to flutter, and as they closed, she pleaded for it to permanent. The last idea crossing her mind was that of the Blue Clicker.

What a blast it would be if she were to die right now in the arms of one of the Seelie Royal Guards. Especially considering a bite or sting of the poisonous beetle should start to take effect any time soon...

All Wahr could think about was what the dandelions was an Unseelie Princess doing on the borderline between the

Seelie and Unseelie lands? Was she not right in the head? Maybe that was what was wrong with her.

She hadn't even spoken a single word as her body became limp. Wahr gently lifted her into his arms. As the Blue Clicker found itself being squished between the hard male body and his armor, it increased its attack biting him multiple times.

Finally, after several attempts to relieve himself of the annoying nipper, it managed to find its way out and up via the neckline of his uniform.

O*n the other side of the veil.*

Tom O'Toole was about to sink his fangs into the succulent neck of the blonde female he'd glamoured into leaving the club with him.

To him, she was just fodder for food,

nothing more than the equivalent to a slab of beef. That's how he saw it. He had been a cow up until three years ago. At first, he found his transformation disgusting, but a blood whore meant he was no longer alone. Hugo had taken a liking to his quick wit and ability to think on the fly, allowing him to move up the ranks faster than that of the dumb and dumber. They'd been growing an army to keep them stronger in numbers. The new ones were not the brightest of soldiers, quickly being turned to dust when they didn't return to the hive before sunrise. Tom was trying to figure out why the juvenile vamps were more zombified than zombies with the collective intelligence of a goldfish.

Movement caught his eye, and he paused in motion to smell the air. The aroma was thick and heavy, like a blow to the head. It made him slightly light-headed and famished at the same time. His stomach growled, and his hands shook. With no explanation for his body's reaction to his environment. He knew it wasn't the blonde, "Stay." He commanded, fixing her in place.

He'd return to her after he placated the sense of impending doom presenting itself as sugar-coated candyfloss. There was something oddly fascinating about the male walking across the street. Tom's eyes narrowed as he leaned his shoulder against the building to watch. He glanced down at the guy's boot as it touched the edge of the grass, an electric sizzle slowly swallowed him. Tom pushed off of the wall, and his eyes widened in disbelief.

Pausing only long enough to give his head a shake, he jogged across the road to stand in the same place the dude had vanished. He studied where the grass and concrete met. Lifting his foot, he moved it to be half on the concrete path and half on the grass. Frowning, he shuffled it sideways first in one direction, then the other. Nothing. No lightning show. No sizzle. And although he could barely smell the faint hint of something which made his fangs hum, he had no idea of what it was that he'd just witnessed. He walked around on the grass for several minutes to confirm there were no hidden trapdoors or Stargates. Returning to where he'd left his feed, he gave a quick surveyance of the area. Satisfied that nobody was watching, he threaded his left hand into the blondes hair to tilt her head back and to the side. His nostrils flared, and he exposed his fangs, holding back a hiss he struck hard and fast, causing the female to gasp. Her hands rose to pull him closer, placing them on his broad shoulders. Tom drank his fill before releasing her. "We came outside for some fresh air. You'd finished your drink and didn't feel very well. You apologized and suggested we catch up another night. Go home."

Tom watched as the female turned to a yellow VW. She pulled the keys from her handbag and pressed the unlock button. Tom spun to focus his attention back to the mystery of the vanishing dude before he ran out of darkness to do it. He surrendered to thoughts of his human life and the way that he wasn't restricted by night and day. He used to get up before the sun. Surf all morning. Get in a couple of hours of work, then head to a bar to shoot pool with the guys. Rinse and do it all over again, at least until Friday night, when it was time to party hard or go home.

After further investigation, he was still no closer to understanding what he'd discovered, instead of coming to the realization that it would have to keep for another day. Tom was not going to waste another minute on it without turning him into a pile of ash if he wasn't in the safety of the hive to avoid the impending rise of the sun. Granted, he was all about the cause but not at his own expense.

As he entered the belly of their den, he knew exactly where to find Hugo before he even looked in the direction of his maker. He found himself wondering if the elder possessed any information that would provide answers to the conundrum that had presented itself to him this evening.

He would need to swear secrecy first,

but something told him it was imperative that he did, regardless of it being his maker or any other bloodsucker. With that mental note, he approached Hugo, greeting him in the same manner as any other uneventful night.

"Did you come across any beasts while you were out to feed?" Hugo asked Tom.

Tom's eyes looked to the right attempting to avoid eye contact with his maker, which in and of itself was a dead giveaway to Hugo that his Tommy was holding back on him. Moving with the speed of an ancient vampire, his hand circled the back of Tom's head, and a fraction of a second later, he sank his fangs into Tom's neck. Tom's memories fed his inquisitive mind while the male's blood fed him sustenance. Images were flashing through his mind of everything that Tom had seen and done. Suddenly he retracted his fangs and embraced Tommy in a hug strong enough to crack mortal bones. "I cannot put a price on what you have given me this night. You will keep this information strictly be-tween the two of us."

"You know what he is?"

"He's fae,"

"What? Like as in a fairy?"

"We will talk about this later. How-ever, I would like for you to go back and watch to see if he returns."

"As you wish, my sire."

As Tom closed his eyes and waited for the day sleep to take him, he wondered if they would miss the visitor if he was to return during the daylight hours when they were unable to watch the spot that the fairy vanished from. He wrinkled his nose. It just didn't seem fitting to label such a massive dude with a name that was usually depicted as cute little femi-nine characters. He recalled being just a kid, and his sister's room was decorated with flowers of purple and pink. Sofia would race home from school to dress in her fairy costume. She would wear little wings and ballet shoes as she fluttered around dancing to music. That's how Tommy liked to remember her. It was the summer just before his mum passed away. Automatically finding distraction with curiosity for why they couldn't share the information, but he did not want to cross Hugo. He knew his maker had created him, and he was well aware he could unmake him quicker than he could turn off a light.

Not wanting to put more energy into his emotions, he focused on what he had to do the next night. He'd begin by returning to Pandemonium and waiting.

CHAPTER 3

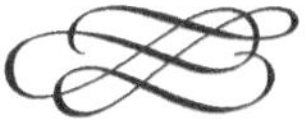

Wahr kicked a pile of leaves below an old elm tree before laying the female down. He collected a multitude of berries and nuts. He usually would have been the one to sit back and allow the females of the courts to serve the culinary delights, or whatever they were called to perform the gathering thing. He looked sideways at the little green misshaped prickles. They were not the most palatable ones, and he wasn't looking to have the Unseelie Princess believe that he was trying to poison her, so he tossed them aside. Adding several of the nearly lily-like flowers onto the top of his peace offering, he wondered how long before the female would wake. It was guilt that prevented him from dropping her off somewhere close to the Unseelie gates, but then he wasn't in the mood for having to explain why she was unconscious. They were on Seelie land after he'd carried her across the border

He didn't possess the answers to the questions they would ask, like why the female was outside the palace gates without an escort.

"Are those for me?"

"Yeah, a peace offering," he shrugged.

Oreo picked up one of the blue ones and popped it into her mouth, it gently imploded against the roof of her mouth, and she struggled to hide a moan of savoring the flavor overload. She swallowed and quickly reached for a different one. "These are spectacular. Are they from your side of the boundary? We don't have anything like them," she looked around, her eyes growing wide as none of her surroundings resembled the land of the Unseelie.

While the sense of fear was genuine, she also felt safe with the Seelie. It was difficult to explain, but he had the chance to kill her, and sadly he'd passed by the opportunity.

Her shoulders slumped forward, and she moved the remainder of the berries and bobbles around on the large leaf.

"Is something wrong? I picked all the edible ones. I avoided any of the poisonous ones. I also excluded any of the mushrooms; some of those can be dangerous."

Before he had sufficient time to react, Oreo plucked the purple shroom to her left and scoffed it into her mouth. She was suddenly on her back with the mammoth Seelie telling her, "Spit it out!" he looked outraged, but she swallowed then opened her mouth to show him that it was gone.

There was no way to return her until the effects of the Loquacious Mushroom wore off. "Snapdragons! Why did you have to go and do that?"

"Why didn't you feed me something

other than delicious fruits and bobbles?" she retorted.

He frowned, "What else would I feed you?"

"Never mind. Now get off of me," Oreo struggled.

Wahr studied the Unseelie female for several seconds. She was truly stunning with her black tattoo's weaving up along her hairline and across her forehead. His initial thought was to trace them with his forefinger. The idea of which was way too personal for strangers to engage in. That was something only a promised could do. His heart beat faster, not with fear but with curious excitement. No other female had ever piqued his interest as such. The Unseelie princess was a puzzle that he wanted to solve, even if it took him a lifetime. And that's when the mushroom kicked in.

"I don't want to return to the Unseelie palace. Please don't make me go back," she all but begged.

Wahr's brow knitted together in confusion, "Why don't you want to go home?" Okay, so Wahr was evil for doing it, but he was going to do it anyway. He planned to use the effects of the mushroom to get to know her. Luckily it was only the mushroom that made them talkative. It was generally used to make their enemy talk when being tortured. They could only speak the truth, and it made them talk without being able to hold back.

Oreo shook her head, trying to stop the words flowing from her mouth, "I refuse to be anchored to likes of Zayton. Not today. Not ever. I would rather cease to exist. I'd gladly become a shadow in the fade of the veil before spending a day with that male. I'd probably end up in the oubliette for doing something forbidden. Although I'm almost positive that he would smother me in my sleep if he thought he could get away with it. You need to get off of me now," she panted. Well aware that at this rate, she would spill her guts in less time than it took to cover her mouth, given that her hands were trapped at her sides.

She narrowed her eyes, "Why are you still on top of me?"

Without warning, Wahr's lips covered hers, and he was kissing her. She momentarily stilled beneath him then opened her mouth to protest. His kiss was hot, and the friction of his lips against hers made a warmth somewhere deep down inside her that she couldn't explain or identify. He made her feel. Her heart sped up to match the speed with which her mind was working.

She liked it. Oreo liked him, but she shouldn't. With that thought, a tear escaped. Her life had just become even more impossibly complicated than it already was. Unseelie and Seelie did not anchor each other, not ever. They were enemies. Oh, and what a beautiful enemy he was. Just because... for no other reason she could invent, she kissed him back. It was like nothing else she had ever experienced. It was a perfect moment. If she were to expire right here, right now, she wouldn't feel as though she had missed out on knowing what it was like to be kissed. He suddenly broke their contact and turned his head to the left. "Someone's coming," he released his hold on her. "Make yourself invisible," he commanded.

Oreo felt a sinking weight in her chest at the thought that he didn't want to be seen with her. While he waited for the intrusion to be complete, she vanished into thin air and ran. With the speed of a sprite, she moved as fast as possible. Leaping over fallen logs, around boulders and rocks and over the black waters of Baggins River. Oreo knew what she didn't want, and now she'd had a taste of what she could never have. With the knowledge that she could barely refrain from vehemently speaking the truth, she aimed to avoid crossing paths with anyone she knew. She snuck into the palace, biting her lower lip painfully to prevent her from muttering to herself as she passed by Zayton's parents. They were arguing over something that was mute in point when it came to her. She'd decided what had to be done, and she would do whatever it took to do it. She continued to weave her way through the palace to reach her chambers. Opening the door carefully, she quietly entered, only to step through and have it slammed behind her.

"Where have you been, daughter of mine?"

"Living a lie," Oreo replied, reappearing in front of her father.

"Your mother's been looking for you," Bryk the Solid growled at his daughter. "Why can't you just do as you're told?"

"Because it's not what I want, even more now than ever before." Oreo lowered her voice to prevent the walls from hearing what they were discussing. "There has to be a way to leave?" she posed the question as a statement in hopes that her father would provide answers to her dilemma. He didn't so much as utter a word, a simple commiseration for her situation. He knew that he was not a love match, and he was miserable in the anchoring between her mother and him. Even so, he gave her nothing she could work with.

"Sit," Bryk advised her. Only after she'd taken the weight off of her feet did he begin. "Legend of the Veil, Elderberry 23:12 explains the coming of the Unseelie. Many eons ago, when the Queen of the Seelie's gave birth to twins, her advisor told her of the great war to come. It was stamped in stone that one day in the future, the twins would divide a civilization. When the twins had reached adulthood, they fell in love with the same male, and it did indeed divided a nation. Nobody thought to ask the male who he loved. He was condemned to be anchored to the eldest born of the twins. He refused to be with the eldest as there was a darkness inside her that he could not connect with. Ivy was the second born twin, and with a broken heart, she left the glade for she was so in love with Onyx the Strong that she could not bear to see him anchored to her sister when she knew he did not feel for her. Velvet, the eldest of the twins, refused to release him, due to her own selfishness, and that cost her not only the inseparable closeness of her twin but also the male she loved. She couldn't bear to know that she was alone and miserable, especially when misery loves company. It was a hard lesson for her to learn, but as a result of her twisted selfishness, her heart turned dark, bringing with it the hatred for the Seelie who would not support her in her desires to hunt them down and sentence them to death. Those that believed the true Queen of the Seelie's was the one who believed she was doing the right thing for her people by walking away followed her. They celebrated the union of Ivy and Onyx. Those who deposed their actions stayed behind with Velvet the violent."

"Oreo, sometimes you have dance to your own music," he sighed. "And sometimes you have to settle for someone else's beat. If you have to dance to another person's rhythm, at least make sure they are willing to also dance to yours from time to time. There is also a legend that speaks of a Bovine Blade. It is designed to be a way to leave the protection of the glade. It is the only safe way for the Seelie and Unseelie alike to travel to the outer world."

"I want what is best for you, and I do not agree with your mother's decision on Zayton's appointment to the Unseelie court. There is something a little off about that male. She may not see it, but it's there," Bryk disclosed his dislike and disapproval for the male.

"So this Bovine blade really does exists, where would I find such a weapon?"

Bryk gave her a slight shake of his head, not trusting that their conversation wasn't being listened to. Instead of answering Oreo, he hugged her, showing her in his mind of where it was last located. It was where he himself had left it many years ago, deep in the bowels of the palace.

"Be blessed, my child." He whispered lovingly.

"Be blessed father," Oreo replied, hugging him back, she wondered if it could be the last time she would ever see him. She silently thanked him using their telepathic connection. Knowing that he wasn't just giving her the secret location of the Bovine Blade, he was giving her a chance to leave the palace for good.

CHAPTER 4

With the Bovine Blade in hand, she returned to the exact place where the Seelie Prince had stepped through the veil. Or at least she was pretty sure it was the spot. Lifting the dagger above her head, she lowered it, stabbing at what looked like nothing to the naked eye. The initial impact scratched the surface, providing confirmation that she had found the veil. It sizzled loudly, and she pulled the blade away from it quickly. Turning in circles, she looked around to see if anyone was watching. When there was no movement, she spun to face the invisible protective wall. Plunging the knife in, she slid it down in one swift motion to open a gateway into the other world. Separating the cut in the veil, she looked through swaying from side to side to check if the doorway was safe to go through. Seeing nothing that stood out as threatening or dangerous, she slipped through the hole sideways without a glance back at the lands of the Unseelie.

Tommy saw the sparks from where he stood to hide in the shadows of Pandemonium. He was ready to move the instant the fae stepped into their world. Only this time, it wasn't the large male he'd seen going through the night before. This time it was a female with tattoos on her face that resembled some sort of vines. She wasn't what he'd expected, but she would do. After all, they were all just a bunch of fairies.

His hand covered her mouth, and his free arm wrapped around her waist. "If you make a sound, I will snap your neck." Tommy threatened to lift her feet off of the ground.

She was at a loss. How did he know she was leaving the glade through the veil?

Tommy felt his teeth zing, and he growled in the back of his throat at how good the female smelled. It was like her blood called to him. He closed his eyes, trying to ignore his desire to sink his fangs in, failing miserably he grazed her neck enough to make it bleed. His mouth watered, and he momentarily felt dizzy. He was at a loss of how to describe the shifting sensations bombarding his entire body. It was so intense he couldn't hold back any longer. His inner beast, the one that he knew was always lurking just beneath the fragments of his fading humanity, took hold of him — pushing him past the point of bloodlust to sink his fangs into the column of the Fae's neck. The taste was beyond anything he'd ever experience before. It was euphoric. The Fae's blood was so pure that it resonated power as it filled his mouth. As if by sheer will alone, he suddenly noticed that the Fae in his arms had gone terribly still.

His high took a rapid dive, Hugo would extinguish him. He'd find himself sentenced to death by sun. Tommy wondered how long the Fae's blood would allow him to walk in the sun before he would burn to death? He sealed the puncture wound on her neck before wrapping his arm around her waist. He was trying not to draw attention to the unconscious female he was escorted back to the secluded safehouse Hugo had set up for occasions such as this.

Not that anything like this had ever happened before now. Which meant the fairy Tommy had in his possession was as rare as hen's teeth, and he'd just proven to his master that he couldn't be trusted not to drain the female to death. The result of his panicked thoughts was to revive her. Not willing to taint her blood with his own, he looked for a dinner where he could garnish some sugar. Hopefully, that would help bring her back. He certainly prayed to the planets, the universe, heaven, and hell that it would work. He wasn't religious, so he had no particular alignment with any church, God, or Goddess. Tommy just wanted one of them to hear his pleas to fix the fairy he'd broken. More importantly, before Hugo discovered what he'd done.

Around the corner from Pandemonium, there was an all-night café, Tommy headed across the street to reach the only place he knew they could find food at this time of night. Doris' Sweet Cherry Pie and Coffee Shop was the epitome of the all-night diners you saw in the movies. He pushed the door open and assisted the Fairy through the doorway. He silently cursed at the overly loud ding from the bell hanging above the door. He would have preferred not to have announced their entrance, never the less he needed to find something to feed the Fairy.

He took up the booth towards the rear. He picked up a menu from the table to hide them behind, aiming for a small reprieve. He just had to try and get the female to eat some sugar. He spilled half of the contents of the first sachet on the table before he could get it to her mouth. The second didn't fare much better, but the third did the trick.

Oreo's eyes flew open, and she licked her lips before her sight focused on the male sitting beside her, and she let loose an ear-piercing screech. At the same time, she spun in her seat and kicked out. Tommy, the vampire, had no idea what semi-trailer had gone flying through the café and reversed over him twice before he hit the wall like splatter paint and slid down to the floor like Teflon.

"If I weren't already dead, then I would be after you attacked me like that," Tommy rubbed the back of his neck as though he still had physical pain. He knew it was phantom pain, but that was something he would theorize over another day and time.

"You tried to kill me," Oreo laid the blame squarely on the male's shoulders, right where it should be. She screwed up her nose at him as if there was something off about his appearance. Recognition clicking into place within her mind, "You're a bloodsucker." She announced loud enough for anyone within earshot to hear.

"In our world, it's not cool to call people names," Tommy explained.

"Well, drain me dry, if you're offended for being called out as a nightwalker, blood-beast, vampire." Oreo shrugged his accusation away as though it were dust on her sleeves. "That's too bad because I'm only just getting started."

"Hey, Tommy," Jacob walked in through the door. His nostrils flared, and he snarled, "What have you gone and found yourself there?"

"Nothing Jacob," Tommy replied, knowing that the female fairy smelled so good that if he didn't get her to the safe house as quickly as possible, then he could lose possession of her.

The bell over the door rang, again and again, to alert them that they were in a precarious situation. Hugo was the last to enter, "Tommy, do we have a problem?"

"No, Sir," Tommy shuffled his foot on

the linoleum. "I was just about to tell Jacob to get out of the way so I could… We could leave." Tommy turned his head to look in the direction of where the fae had been standing her ground. Only she wasn't there anymore. He turned in a complete circle three times to locate where she'd gone.

The overly loud ding of the front door to the café gave cause for everyone to turn to see who was coming or going.

Oreo made herself invisible the moment the opportunity arose. With the stealth of an experienced Unseelie Court Guard, she moved silently through the café to avoid so much as a slight brush against any of the bloodsuckers slowly increasing in numbers.

When Tommy looked past the gathering horde, he knew it had to be the female fae escaping as nobody was coming into the café, and nobody was walking out.

"Stop her!" he cried.

Hugo wrapped her hair around his closed fist and tugged her back inside.

Wahr stood to the right of the throne where his mother's royal tush sat. Her posture was that of the Queen about to be confronted by the enemy. The Seelie Court had been presented with a blooded coat of arms from the Unseelie Queens Court.

"Is there a reason for them to believe that we took the Unseelie Princess?"

"No, mother. Their claims are unfounded," he responded.

"Then tell me then son of mine, why when you have the name that puts fear into the hearts of both Seelie and Unseelie alike would that they still make this accusation, regardless of the consequences?" the Seelie Queen asked.

"My name does not define me, but if they want war, then I will be happy to incite it. It will be on my terms and my timeline." Wahr offered. "Has anyone taken into consideration that the Unseelie Princess doesn't want to be sentenced by her parents to be anchored to a soggy lily leaf such as Zayton?"

"How would you know of the politics of the Unseelie Court. Unless…"

"Fine, I freely admit that I may have bumped into the Unseelie Princess recently as I returned from one of my outings."

"I strongly suggest that if you have any idea where the princess may be hiding, that you find her and return her to her people."

"So, it has nothing to do with whether she is happy or not?" Wahr folded his arms over his chest to question his mother. "Would you have me anchored to a female who cannot hold my interest?"

"We will discuss that when you get back." She scolded.

"No. We will talk about it now."

"You will be anchored to the most suitable female of the Seelie Court."

"Absolutely not! Don't push me on this mother, or you will regret it."

"I forbid you to be anchored to the likes of your father's people."

"I didn't ask for any of this. And I refuse to be a puppet or pawn in your game of wills against my father. I suggest you figure that out sooner rather than later." Wahr stepped down from beside his mother's throne and walked with his shoulders back, emanating the visual perfection of a future king. His mother studied his back as he exited the room. Disappointment etched within her beauty. She had hoped he would at least look back over his shoulder. The hand she had raised to wave to her departing son, dropped to her lap and tears escaped. She didn't want to be the ogre, but at the 'End of Fall' party, her son was to be anchored. It was politics. It was a historical event. It was the law. She had to make things right. The sour taste in her mouth reminded her that she herself had broken those laws by falling in love with a God. She had not given any thought to the overall outcome of having a child out of anchorage, but then to have given her heart to a different type of being was unforgivable. Her son's words were something to make her pause and consider her own future. Did she really want to be Queen of the Seelie if it meant she couldn't be true to herself and love who she wanted to love?

Wahr returned to where he'd last seen the Unseelie Princess searching both sides of the boundary. As he was about to give up, a glimmer from something caught his eye. The dagger looked to be embedded in... 'Oh snapdragons!'

When he touched the blade to remove it from the fragile fold of the veil, it sparked images inside his mind. It was replaying what had transpired. Wahr saw the Unseelie Princess cut through the thin layer of the veil, followed by a struggle on the other side. He could only guess that someone had captured her, but for what purpose? Tucking the Bovine

Blade into his boot, he stepped free of the glade straight through the veil, which sealed itself as though it were the surface of a pool of water expelling an air bubble. Immediately cloaking his wares, he walked across the road, from there the instant he stepped over the curb, his boot faltered with an electric pull away from Pandemonium, towards the corner of the street. Following the Bovine Blades energetic hum, he walked in that direction. At the intersection, he spied the signage of an all-night diner and knew that the Unseelie Princess had gone that way. Still allowing the blade to lead him to the female's location, he entered Doris' Sweet Cherry Pie and Coffee Shop. The place was empty except for the waitress who could pass for being Doris herself. Wahr approached the woman without drawing her attention. He wondered why the bell above the door hadn't been enough to warrant a glance from her? It wouldn't matter, as Wahr would ensure that he wasn't even a blink in her timeline. Touching her temple, he accessed her memories, only to hit a mind block. Odd wasn't even the right word for it. He wanted to dive deeper, but then considering the woman's age, he didn't want her to stroke out, so he rejected the idea.

Exiting the diner the same way he had entered, the blade hummed against his lower leg. When he took a step to the right, the humming stopped making him pause. He glared down at the hilt protruded from his boot and narrowed his eyes at the finicky hand weapon. "Really?" he vocalized, then shook his head at the notion that he was communicating with an inanimate object. Looking around to see if he was being watched, he was relieved to note there was no one else around. The skies of the otherworld were beginning to bleed through the darkness. It provided a warning of the pending new day as it grew closer. The time difference between both worlds made him sluggish as he followed the resident buzz in his boot. Wahr had reached a rhythmic jogging pace when without any forewarning or advance notification, the dagger ceased to be anything more than a weapon. No guidance given. Wahr glanced around at his surroundings and realized he had no idea where he was. Being geographically challenged was the least of his concerns at this point in time. His bigger problem being the whereabouts of the Unseelie Princess. He shouldn't care, but something inside his chest told him that he did. Whether he wanted to or not. Performing a mental calculation, he concluded that the Unseelie Princess would have been in the otherworld for what would equate to five days. With no further guidance in the correct direction to locate the Princess, he turned in a slow-motion circle to look for any nuances to provide prompting as to his next step in finding the female.

Hugo and Tommy both drank from the Fae's veins, Tommy from her right wrist and Hugo from her left.

They'd been getting more and more aggressive with their attempts to withstand the sun. The first day they had access to the Fae's blood, they'd managed to watch the sunrise before feeling sensitive to its rays. The second day they had managed to not only see the sunrise, but they'd stood before its rays for a good ten minutes before their skin began to singe and blister. Each day since had enabled them to remain outside as a day-walker for a growing amount of time. Although they were famished for the Fae's blood, they never seemed to be able to get enough. The more they drank, the more they wanted until they were almost feral from bloodlust. Their eyes were bloodshot, and they wore pink panda rings around them, and their fangs no longer receded. While the others had initially fought one another to take a bite out of the Fae. They were now all extinguished, and there was only Hugo and Tommy left at the safe house. They weren't able to think about anything except the power of the Fae's blood. It made them feel invincible.

The younger ones of the horde were unable to sustain past the first day. They had developed cold-like symptoms within the first two hours of taking the vein of the Fae. Several of them managed to defy their fate for a few more hours, but they were not of Hugo's lineage. Sadly, not even the undead can avoid the truth… The Unseelie Princess's blood was poison to them.

CHAPTER 5

Oreo was floating somewhere between the otherworld and the Fade. She could no longer care if she ever saw the glade again. She'd left. She'd chosen not to stay where it was safe all so she wouldn't have to be anchored to Zayton, the bottom feeder. If she'd had the energy, she would have laughed at her mental debasement of the male that thought he would one day be the King of the Unseelie Court. 'Not today, Zayton.' She gave an internal smirk at messing with the egotistical, pompous, bubble blowers self-appointed future. 'Not ever.'

He was so full of hot air he frothed at

the mouth whenever he became agitated. Not to mention if someone said, 'No.' to him.

She was no longer hot or cold. Her body was most likely in some state of shock, but once again, she didn't seem to be able to accumulate enough energy to care past her next breath. The last thing she pictured in her mind as she drifted away was the strong features of the Seelie Prince. Her heart stuttered as he leaned over her, his mouth was moving, but she couldn't hear or understand what he was saying to her. Oreo knew she'd gone beyond the point of returning from the grey. It surrounded her, swallowed her until she couldn't tell where she began or where the fifty shades of grey ended…

Wahr could feel the urgency deep down inside his chest. Fear. Pure unadulterated fear. He'd never experienced anything like it before. The sense of losing something before ever having the chance to learn it's intricacies. All he could think about was that he was going soft. He shook his head to clear his thoughts of hearts and flowers. The image of the Unseelie Princess lying on the bed of leaves on the ground beneath him made his lips tingle. His eyes snapped open. He hadn't even realized he'd closed them. He wasn't going to question why he'd done it. He knew why it was to find her. Wahr felt as though he couldn't draw a breath. His hearing was the first thing to go. Breathing through his nose, he inhaled deeply. Wahr had always been in touch with his powers as the Seelie Prince. Now, he reached into a part of himself he barely knew, except something told him to bend his knee to become one with the earth, the universe, and the gods. He placed his palm flat. Tendrils of energy reached out seeking, searching for the Unseelie Princess' signature. The one he'd tasted on her lips. was the one female that drew his interest. Her floral scent. He searched his surroundings for even the most infinite indication that she was close by.

As two males walked out of a house to his left, one of his sensory tentacles connected with the faintest of energy sources making his heart falter. It was so fragile it terrified him that he was too late to save her. Before he knew it, his feet were moving him towards the men that were exiting the two-story dwelling, which blended into the other suburban houses on the street. Nothing screamed that there was a Fae Princess inside. Regardless, he knew she was. She had to be. The closer he got to the two males, the blade began to vibrate so hard it was emanating a high pitched sound. Both of the men dropped to their knees, putting their hands over their ears, bowing forward they exhibited signs of being in excruciating pain.

"Make it stop!" Tommy cried out. "Please make it stop!" he begged.

Wahr removed the blade from where it was, and with the sure hand of a warrior, he plunged it into the chest of the vampire ending his suffering perma-nently. Hugo moved his hands from where they protected his ears to wave them in surrender in front of himself. Wahr moved past him, too desperate to reach the fading Unseelie Princess.

Kicking the door open, he raced in-side. Once inside, it was as though he were drawn towards her. She was in the cooking area of the dwelling. She looked paler than he remembered from the first time he'd seen her amongst the leaves.

He wanted to see her that way again one day. Without giving it a second thought, he used the Bovine Blade to slice across his palm. He replicated his movements cutting Oreo's palm to match his. Quickly slapping them together be-fore their flesh could heal, he spoke in his native tongue barely above a whisper the ancient ritual of the Seelie. "Amin blood, naa llea blood. Amin breath naa llea breath. Amin life naa llea life while oio allae live." [Translation - My blood is your blood. My breath is your breath. My life is your life while ever I live.] "I will fight for you, and I'll fight beside you. I will anchor you, and you will anchor me."

Wahr rested his forehead against the Unseelie Princess's hand, where they were joined, and he made all manner of promises to keep her safe. Standing, he leaned over her. He believed she was still with him, but only barely. Wanting to complete the ceremony, he leaned down to bestow a gentle kiss on her soft pink lips. As he moved to separate their lips, Oreo tentatively returned the feather-light caress of her lips against his.

Oreo felt a warm sensation seeping down her reaching all the way to her toes. It was as if she were cocooned in one of her father larger than life hugs. Only it was from a heat signature she couldn't instantly recognize from the distance of the Fade. Slowly the grey engulfing her became paler, thinner, cleaner, and more white. Something told her she should know the energy blanketing her was offering her a future she would want, a future that promised love, understanding, and devotion from a male worthy of being a Fae of Nobility.

Wahr searched the Unseelie Princess's features as her eyes fluttered open. "Hi," his voice sounded gruff, but it was purely unintentional.

"Um," Oreo offered in a hoarse throat. "What are you doing here?"

"I came to find you."

"Why?"

"Because the Unseelie Court believe that we took you," he admitted.

"I'm so sorry," she offered. "I didn't mean for that to happen."

"I know," Wahr acknowledged. "I see no logic in doing what you did other than to avoid being anchored to the male you were not willing to be saddled with."

"I can't go back," Oreo stated. "I won't go back."

"You'd refuse to return to the glade even knowing that you could die if you stay in the otherworld?"

"Yes," she confirmed.

"Good thing your parents no longer have a say in who anchors you now," the right side of Wahr's lips turned up in a sexy smirk.

Oreo frowned at the Seelie Prince's words, not understanding what he was saying. As every minute passed by, the Unseelie Princess grew stronger, more revived. Wahr traced his forefinger along the Unseelie Princess' tattoos, making the black inked patterns swirl with iridescent colors. He watched as they replaced the solid dark lines transforming her beauty into something unmeasurable on a physical level.

"You take liberties that are not yours to take. I am Oreo. The Princess of the Unseelie Court." She lifted her chin in a show of defiance.

"I vow to protect you with my life," Wahr promised. "But we need to prove to your mother that you are alive and well. The Unseelie Court needs to know that you are not being held in our vine chambers against your will."

With a sigh, she conceded that it wasn't right to leave the glade on the brink of war. However, she couldn't guarantee if she would stay.

~

Wahr watched as Oreo transformed before his eyes. She'd sent word to her parents that she was alive and well. She told them that her location would not be disclosed at this time, but she was taking some time to get her head straight before announcing her own choice in anchorage.

Some of the changes were minuscule, and others were monumental. Oreo's tattoos transforming at Wahr's touch was fascinating to watch. It was intimate and personal. Oreo's eyelids fluttered closed as Wahr's fingers caressed the path of her tattoos from her temple down the side of her cheek, all the way down her neck and over her shoulder. Her hair had light blonde strips through it as it changed in color.

Wahr held her in arms encompassing her with his warmth. Today being the day the Unseelie Court had sent out the invitations. He kissed Oreo brushing his lips against hers. Her hands rested against Wahr's naked chest, and she still found it a surprise that he had convinced her to stay. She had initially tried to run, but no matter where she hid, he found her. She would feel the energy around her shimmer briefly before he would appear before her, kissing her tenderly. Eventually, she gave up trying as she no longer wanted to leave him. Her Seelie Prince was the male that her heart belonged to. It probably had something to with the fact that he'd tied them together. If she were to return to the glade, it would be with him. It was just like her father had told her. She had always hoped she would find someone to dance with, and now she had. Now it was time for them to tell her parents.

Wahr had returned to the Seelie Court to find that his mother and father had come to an arrangement. His mother sat on her throne, and his father stood to her left. The room was buzzing with sharp tongues and evil eyes as the Unseelie Queen and King were escorted to their seats. The Unseelie Queen lifted her nose in the air to indicate that she was above the general population of the Seelie Court.

"What are all the theatrics for?" Heliconia sneered at her anchored.

"Hel you will be pleasant, even if it kills you," Zephyr put the Queen of the Unseelie in her place.

Wahr spoke above the hum filling the gathering space, "My chosen has requested that we all be present for the following announcement as it affects Seelie and Unseelie alike." He looked to his right as Oreo stepped out from behind the ivy curtains. She only had eyes for Wahr. He lifted his hand in greeting, as she reached him, he placed a kiss to her lips. "I am Wahr born of Ezla the Seelie Queen and Zion of the Gods. This is Oreodaphne born of Heliconia and Zephyr, the King and Queen of the Unseelie Court. Today is the day that Seelie and Unseelie become one once more.

There will no longer be divination between us. Only unity will exist within the walls of the Glade. If you are not willing to become one nation, then you will be more than free to leave."

Wahr held Oreo's hand and encouraged her to take a seat beside his mother.

Wahr retained hold of Oreo's hand as his mother stood and turned to stand at a ninety-degree angle to Oreo's seat. She raised her voice, "Do you accept what is offered of my own free will?"

"I do," Oreo answered nervously, trying not to look at Wahr. She wanted him to be proud of his decision.

"Then rise to the challenge," Ezla smiled at her son, giving him a wink. Oreo rose from her seat to stand, her head fitting into the crown of thorns. Her shoulders straightened, and her chin lifted with the air of royalty.

Gathering herself, Oreo spoke a few words of warning to provide clarity on the situation, "For those of you who are considering the option to leave, I wish to forewarn you that you will be removed from the Glade and expelled to the otherworld. There are dangers outside the Glade that you couldn't even imagine," she leveled her eyes on those of her father's. It is not safe, and should the creatures beyond the veil ever find a way to cross into our world. We will need to stand together if we are to defeat them."

Zayton stepped free of the group, "You are promised to me," he accused, pointing his finger at Oreo.

"Perhaps in your mind, but that was never going to happen, and in fact, I told you this so many times, I started to think you were suffering from eating too many honey bugs." Oreo turned to Wahr and asked in a whisper, "Is it against the Laws of Seelie to eat them, as they are an endangered species?" Wahr gave her a nod of affirmation.

"You're so basic," Zayton countered defensively.

Wahr stepped forward, "I resent your reference to my Anchored and my Queen as basic. She is definitely not as generically challenged as you are, and for your insult, I could have you encased in ice and gifted to the Bogans of Ippyswich."

"The divination of your nations is no longer, and all will bend the knee for the new Seelie King and Queen," Zion father of Wahr declared, wrapping his arm around the waist of the only female he would ever love with all of his heart.

The first to throw his cloak over his shoulder and to bend his knee was the proudest father in all of the Glade, "My Queen," he bowed his head as a sign of respect before repeating himself to honor his daughters Anchored.

"Get up, you fool," Heliconia snarled.

"If you know what is good for you, then you too will get down here next to me, or I will apply to the King and Queen to have our Anchorage dispelled.

He watched Heliconia gasp in shock, "You wouldn't?"

"Refuse me and see."

Although they were not a love match, Heliconia had grown to love Zephyr. Without so much as another word, she lowered gracefully to her knees beside her Anchored. Following his example, she bowed her head, first to Wahr and then to Oreo. Zephyr took Heliconia's hand, lifting it to his lips, he kissed her knuckles. "Look at our daughter. She is no longer Unseelie."

Wahr stepped closer to his Queen, "Just say the word, and I will have him gift-wrapped in a bow."

"You wouldn't?" Oreo smiled.

"For you, my Queen, I would do anything."

Oreo narrowed her eyes on her King, "Anything?"

She lifted up on her tip-toes and whispered in his ear.

"Really?" he frowned with a sly smile.

Oreo nodded, "As serious as Pickle-Winkles."

"You know how to make Pickle-Winkles?"

With a firm nod of his head, he whisked his Anchored away from the crowded Seelie Court. A short time later, they could be found dancing in the middle of the dancefloor of Pandemonium. The music blared around them, and they stood stock still holding each other close. They refused to dance to anyone else's rhythm because they had discovered that they preferred to dance to their own beat, together.

The End

ABOUT THE AUTHOR

Melissa Bell is an author from Brisbane, Australia. She is a Paranormal Romance author, and this is a Young Adult (PG+) Fantasy Romance, and this is her first publication in the genre.